How To

FIGHT A GIRL

How To
FIGHT A GIRL
Thomas Rockwell

Illustrated by
Nick Sharratt

ORCHARD BOOKS

ORCHARD BOOKS
96 Leonard Street, London EC2A 4RH
Orchard Books Australia
14 Mars Road, Lane Cove, NSW 2066
ISBN 1 86039 347 0 (paperback)
This edition published 1996
A CIP catalogue record for this book is available from
the British Library.
Printed in Great Britain by
The Guernsey Press Company Ltd, Guernsey, Channel Islands

Contents

1 Instant Gangrene

Alan gazed down at the rut the trail bike had made in the mud in front of his sneakers. Billy had almost run over him. There were even tiny splashes of mud on his sneakers. Billy was always showing off. "He ate fifteen worms," muttered Alan to himself in a sarcastic voice. "And so he won the *bet*, wah wah. And then he traded the minibike for the trail bike, so now he's a big *deal*." Alan wiped the splashes of mud off his sneakers. If he could just think of some way to get back at Billy – like some way to make Billy's parents think Billy had taken the trail bike out on the road, so they'd take it away from him. Maybe they'd even make him sell it.

Alan turned and watched Billy gunning the

trail bike up the muddy track through the field. He began to gnaw his fingernail – a thin, red-haired boy with a pale, smudged face, his shirt-tail hanging out, his glasses mended with tape. There had to be some way. He stopped biting his fingernail. And then he clutched his face over his glasses with both hands and yelled:

"He ran over my *feet*! My toes are all *broken*!"

He fell to his knees in the hay and daisies.

At the top of the rise Billy stopped the trail bike and looked back. Alan had yelled something? Now he was kneeling in the hay holding his face? Joe was still back behind the stone wall, burning the lunch papers. Billy took off his crash helmet. The trail bike couldn't have *touched* Alan; he'd just steered close enough to scare him a little.

Alan collapsed slowly down into the hay, still clutching his face.

"What's the matter?" yelled Joe.

Suddenly Billy felt all hollow and weak inside, a lump in his throat. He dropped the crash helmet and started back down the track towards

Alan, slipping and sliding. Joe scrambled over the wall and ran up the other way. They both stopped before they got to Alan.

"What happened?" asked Joe.

Neither of them could see Alan in the hay.

"I didn't get anywhere near him," said Billy.

"You mean you ran over him?" Joe edged closer, trying to see over a clump of daisies. He was a small, wiry, dark-complexioned boy with black hair and a big nose. He found a stick in the hay and poked Alan with it a few times before he realised Alan was only pretending.

"It doesn't look like rigor mortis has set in yet." Joe glanced at Billy – he was really upset, his face all red. "But geez, you know, there is this rotten smell. He must be turning to *gangrene*."

Billy felt as if he couldn't breathe. "Gangrene doesn't happen that fast."

"Come on, you've never heard of *instant gangrene*? Like instant mashed potatoes."

Joe leaned down and lifted Alan's shoulder a little. His eyes were closed, his glasses hanging off one ear.

"Muzzer," Alan moaned faintly. "Muzzer. Feed all clushed."

"We better carry him down to your house."

They got his arms over their shoulders, put his glasses back on. His legs were all rubbery. His feet kept turning in like a cripple's. His head lolled on his chest. He was drooling.

"Boy," panted Joe, "I'm glad I'm not you."

Billy kept wanting to drop Alan and run. Every time Alan's head touched his cheek, he remembered how people's hair keeps growing even after they die. He couldn't believe it had *happened*. They'd just been fooling around like always. If Alan didn't die, he'd let him ride the trail bike whenever he wanted – he'd give him his extra Kawasaki shoulder patch. It must have been *partly* Alan's fault; like he'd stuck his foot out to try and tip the trail bike over. The bike could have crashed. He, Billy, could have been really injured.

Joe was ducking out from under Alan's arm. Alan swung around like a door and clawed at Billy's clothes. Billy frantically pushed him off, almost falling.

Alan knelt on his hands and knees on the path, his head hanging down like a sick dog's.

"He was too heavy," said Joe. "I'd better run for help."

When he got to the barns, he stopped and yelled back, "Don't worry. I'm your friend, too. I won't say you did it unless they make me".

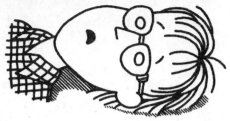

2 The Zombie

First one of Alan's arms collapsed, then the other, so just his rear end was sticking up at Billy. Billy couldn't tell if he was still breathing. But then he realised your rear end probably doesn't move when you breathe, so . . .

"Alan?" he whispered. "Alan?"

Alan rolled over on to his back, his arms flopping out, and his *eyes*! his eyes were Zombie eyes, only the whites showing!

But Billy could see he was still breathing.

"If – if he doesn't die," he whispered, "I'll – I'll *give* him the trail bike."

Alan sat up.

"Okay, hand over the key."

3

Billy was so surprised at first that he didn't understand what had happened. He'd heard of corpses sitting up suddenly in their coffins – but saying "Hand over the key"? Alan's glasses glinted opaquely in the sunlight like a mad scientist's.

"Come on," Alan said. "You said you'd give me the trail bike if I was all right, so I'm all right." He got up.

Billy realised Alan had been faking all along. He hadn't been hurt at all.

"*Yeah?*" Billy yelled. He'd *cream* Alan! He wouldn't even mind kicking him in the *face*! **"YEAH?"** His fists were clenched; he was panting. **"YEAH?"** But he still didn't jump Alan. He knew if Alan lost his temper he'd do anything. He didn't care. Once Alan's mother had bawled him out and then started back to the house, and when she'd gotten about ten feet away, Alan had all of a sudden punched out at her so hard he'd fallen down. And then he'd scrambled up with a rock in each hand and thrown them, not right *at* her exactly, but at least sort of in her direction sideways. And now he was hunching his shoulders up and squinting at Billy with his chin stuck out.

"Cheater. Cheater."

But Alan really felt almost like he wanted to cry. He knew he wouldn't have a chance against big, fat, ugly Billy. "Cheater. You wouldn't care if my glasses broke and I got blinded."

Billy realised Alan was scared. "So take them off."

"Yeah. Yeah, so then I won't be able to see and you can really get me."

Billy shoved him. "What's the matter, Alan? You scared?"

Behind Billy, down the hill, Alan saw Billy's mother come around the corner of the barn. Joe was running beside her, pointing. Alan charged into Billy with his head down, grabbing him around the middle. Billy fell over backwards with Alan's head boring into his stomach. He punched at him. Alan wouldn't let go. Then Billy's mother was standing over them, yelling, "Billy! Alan!"

They both stopped struggling.

"Alan, get off Billy."

Alan started to back off, covering his head with his hands in case Billy tried to get in a sneak punch. Then he remembered he was supposed to have been run over. He hesitated, all bent over. Then he collapsed on to his side, clutching the ends of his sneakers, groaning. Billy tried to kick at him. His mother pulled him away.

4 Black Eggs

But when Billy tried to tell her what had really happened, Alan sat up and started yelling and acting obnoxious. Joe kept saying behind Billy's mother,

"I don't care. He didn't promise to give *me* his trail bike. It doesn't make any difference to me if Billy wants to be a liar. I don't care."

Finally Billy's mother lost her temper and said that was *enough*! she didn't want to *hear* any more. "*Stop it! All of you!* Alan and Joseph, you go home! Do you hear me? Home. I'm going to call your mothers. *Joseph! Stop it!* I don't want to hear any more!" She grabbed his shoulder and turned him around. "Do you hear me? Now go."

She and Billy watched them go down the path toward the barns. Alan was still pretending to limp. Then she turned to Billy and said, "Give me the key".

He gave it to her.

"Now go get the motorcycle and put it in the garage."

"Mom, it's not a motorcycle," said Billy. "It's a trail bike."

But that only made things worse. She screamed, "BILLY!" But then she took a deep breath and said very quietly,

"Billy. Put it in the garage. This is the end of it. I told Daddy what would happen. Now it is *the end.*"

So Billy said okay.

And then he took off his motorcycle racer's gloves and elbow pads and handed them to her in the crash helmet.

She was standing crooked because she had only one slipper on; she'd lost the other running up through the orchard.

"Do you want me to look for your slipper for you?" Billy asked.

She started to limp back towards the barns. "Just go get the motorcycle."

But she looked as if she'd calmed down a little. Billy felt desperate; she'd said it was the *end*.

"Mom, nothing really happened. Alan was faking. I didn't really run over him."

She stopped and looked around at him.

"Oh. So you missed him? Really? So if we just give you another chance, you'll make sure next time?"

Billy went to get the trail bike. When his mother got sarcastic, even his father just let her win. He'd shrug and say something like "Yeah, well". And then he'd motion to Billy and his little sister, Janie, to just eat the scrambled eggs, even if they were all burned black.

5 The Smear

Going home, Alan began to boast how, boy, he'd tricked Billy so bad; his mother would probably take the trail bike away forever.

Finally Joe told him if he didn't shut up, he'd punch him.

"What are you getting so upset for?" said Alan.

"I'm not getting upset," said Joe. "You are. You really think Billy's mother's going to take away the dumb bike? Did she ever do anything the whole time with the worms? She just lets him do whatever he wants."

They went on along the sidewalk.

"If you really wanted to get Billy, you'd have to think up some plan," said Joe.

"Like what?" said Alan. He still thought he'd sort of got Billy, but Joe was probably right about Billy's mother.

"Well, like what's the worst thing that could happen to someone?"

"Getting run over by a truck?"

"Come on. Not like that. Something that's embarrassing, so everybody laughs at you, thinks you're stupid."

"Oh. Yeah."

Alan thought of like waking up in the middle of Yankee Stadium with no clothes on. But Joe probably didn't mean like that either. They went up the steps into Joe's house.

"You want a soda?"

Joe remembered the time the captain of the high-school cheerleaders, Boom Boom Davidson, had started showing off on the late bus, pretending he was her sweetie, trying to kiss and hug him.

They got sodas from the refrigerator and started upstairs to Joe's room. Voices were coming from his sister Rena's room.

"A little more purple here."

14

"Now you do me."

Joe recognised Amy Miller's voice. She and Rena were probably putting makeup on each other. Billy had pretended Boom Boom Davidson had gotten lipstick on Joe's cheek. He stopped. Alan bumped against him.

"What – "

"Wait. I got it. You got any money?"

6 Only Four Days

Billy's mother washed her foot in the kitchen sink, lecturing Billy about friendship. Friendship meant sharing and thinking about your friend's feelings; Alan had lost the bet about the worms and Billy had got the motorcycle, so Billy should try especially hard to be nice to his friend.

Billy kept wanting to ask about the trail bike, but he knew he'd better not. So he just sat at the kitchen table, playing with the sugar spoon and saying yeah. "Yeah, that's like what Mrs Presser says sometimes in school."

The phone rang. It was Billy's father. He wanted to bring some clients home for a drink.

Billy helped his mother cut up cucumbers and little triangles of toast, went to get Emily from her friend's house, wiped off the furniture around the pool with a damp sponge.

"Good," said his mother finally, surveying the two plates of hors d'oeuvres, the tray of glasses and napkins.

"Maybe I ought to go out and wipe off my trail bike," said Billy. "In case any of the clients want to look at it."

"Your trail bike?" said his mother. Then she laughed. "All right. You've helped out, so we'll only make it four days. No riding for four days."

7 The Orange-Juice Moustache

But that night after supper, while Billy was drying the dishes, Emily came into the kitchen and said, "There's a girl who wants to see Billy".

Billy went down the hall to the front door. A girl was standing on the porch.

"Hi, Billy," she said.

At first Billy didn't recognise her through the screen door, but then he realised it was Amy Miller, a girl from his class. But she looked different. It wasn't just the screen. She was all made-up: green-black-silvery slanty eyes, dark purply lipstick, a big spot of crimson on each cheek, her blonde hair all in ringlets like an old-fashioned girl.

"Hi," he said. What could she want? She was in his class but he didn't *know* her. She was supposed to be like the prettiest girl in the class. But with the weird makeup she looked sort of like two people at once: Miss Disco Weirdo from a video and, at the same time underneath that, still Amy Miller from Mrs Presser's class at school.

"Can you come out?" she said.

"What for?"

It was sort of like her head was too big, like it didn't go with the rest of her. She had on a *Chorus Line 2000* red T-shirt.

"Oh. I just wanted to talk to you." She flapped her arms up and down.

"Billy, why don't you ask your friend to come in?" His mother came up the hall from the kitchen and went into the living room.

"Do you want to come in?" said Billy.

"Oh." Amy flapped her arms again.

"Billy, I'm surprised at you." His mother unhooked the screen door. "Come in, dear. He's not really a savage. Boys just act that way sometimes."

Amy came in.

"Why don't you two go sit in the living room?" said his mother. "I'll bring you some juice and cookies."

Billy almost said it's not a party. But his mother would probably say something sarcastic. He waited until he heard the kitchen door shut. Amy had gone into the living room and was looking at the picture over the fireplace.

"So. What?" he said.

Amy flapped her arms without turning around. "Oh, I just wanted to talk to you."

Now it was like she was *three* people, Billy thought: Miss Disco Weirdo, ordinary Amy Miller, and a big bird. He'd never had anything to do with her in school. She was supposed to be a friend of Joe's sister, Rena. Billy decided he'd better do something before Mom came back, so he sat down on the couch and picked up a magazine. The kitchen door squeaked. Emily came into the living room with two glasses of orange juice and some cookies on a tray. Amy and Billy each took a glass and a cookie. Emily put the tray down on the coffee table and left.

Billy pretended to be reading something interesting in the magazine. But then he heard a noise. He looked up.

Amy was sitting on the other couch, looking at him with this huge orange-juice moustache all over her top lip.

"Oh," she said, affectedly cocking her head on one side when she saw him looking at her, "doesn't orange juice always remind you of screwdrivers?"

Billy stared at her. Maybe she was crazy, like an insane person.

But then she began to talk about other cocktails she'd tasted, and Billy remembered a screwdriver was a cocktail made with orange juice. She laughed. The best place to sneak tastes of drinks was at grown-up dances. Didn't Billy think so? That was so much fun. If Billy wanted, he could come to the Fourth of July Dance at the Tennis Club with her.

She bent down over the plate of cookies on the coffee table and began to lick her finger and pick up the crumbs with it and eat them, her mind racing: she shouldn't have come; it was stupid;

why had she let Rena and her brother persuade her?

Billy realised she'd probably just been acting weird because she'd been nervous about asking him to the dance.

"You mean you want me to take you to the Fourth of July Dance?" he said. Girls were always thinking about mush and stuff like that; like girls always wanted square dancing instead of basketball in gym.

She looked up at him with her green-black-silvery slanty eyes and big orange-juice moustache. "Yes."

"I can't," said Billy, grinning. "I'm taking my grandmother."

"Your grandmother?"

"Yeah." Billy jumped up. "She may be old and wrinkly, but boy, can she disco."

. And he pretended to disco, waving his arms and jumping around singing "Boop-boop de-boop."

Amy stood up abruptly, banging her shins against the coffee table so it rattled. Then she tripped over it. She almost ran to the door. But she couldn't get the screen door open. She pulled and yanked.

Billy was still discoing behind her. "Boop-boop de-boop."

Amy let go of the handle and took a deep breath. She tossed her head back. Then she put both hands carefully on the handle, pushed down while she pulled, then pushed up while she pulled. She got frantic again, yanking, pulling. Finally she pushed out without realising it, the door flew open, and she almost fell out on to the porch.

Billy started to call boop-boop after her as she ran down the steps. But then he didn't.

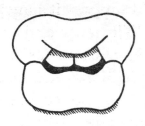

8 Mushed Lips

At breakfast the next morning Billy's mother slammed open the cabinet under the sink and dumped the plate of pancakes into the garbage can.

"There. Is that what you want?" she said to Billy's father.

"Eleanor, I was only making a joke."

The sunlit kitchen was silent, Emily and Billy watching to see what their mother was going to do next. Billy didn't even dare set down his empty orange-juice glass; the least sound or movement might set off another explosion.

"Eleanor, I really was only making a joke," said his father finally.

His mother set the plate in the sink and turned

on the water full blast. The front doorbell rang. No one moved.

"I suppose it's my job to answer that, too?"

"Billy, answer the door," said his father.

As Billy pushed open the swinging door into the hall, his mother threw the dish sponge into the sink, so he knew she wasn't finished yet; sometimes lately you couldn't even tell what had made her lose her temper. Billy glanced ahead down the hall and gasped: a weird, misshapen face was peering in at him through the screen.

"Boy, that Amy Miller's so dumb," said the face.

Billy realised it was someone with his face mushed against the screen door.

"I hate her so much," said the face. "She thinks she's so great." The voice got all smarmy. "*Billy*, will you take *me* to the dance because *I'm so pretty* and everything?"

Billy realised it was Rena, Joe's sister.

"We can make her look so stupid. I've got this plan. I'll pay you if you help. Okay?"

Billy licked his lips. Rena was mad at Amy? Why was she mashing her face against the screen? She wasn't as pretty as Amy. She wasn't fat or anything, but she looked sort of like a giant had put his hand on her head and squashed her a little.

"I have to go," he said. He gestured back at the kitchen. "I'm helping my father."

She was almost scary. It *hurt* when you pressed your face that hard against a screen.

"But we could get her so easy."

Now she couldn't even talk straight. Her lips were glooged back so the wet pink part showed. Billy glanced behind him to see if the kitchen door was open and caught sight of himself in the mirror over the hall table – with this huge orange-juice moustache all over his upper lip!

"I – I have to go."

In the kitchen his father suddenly yelled, "Eleanor!"

"See," said Billy. "My father's calling me."

"Your name isn't Eleanor," said the squashed face.

Billy just turned and went back up the hall. He could feel the face watching him. The kitchen door swung shut behind him. He sat down at the table and picked up his orange-juice glass. Then he put it down and carefully wiped all around his mouth. He'd thought Amy was weird because of her orange-juice moustache. Mom and Dad were still arguing, but now they were arguing about stuff he and Emily weren't supposed to know, so he couldn't even understand what they were arguing about.

"What about *last week*," said his mother, "when you did what we talked about *yesterday*? What about that? Oh, that's *nothing*, that's not important, that's a wife's *duty*."

"You can bring that up now?" said his father. He glanced at Billy and Emily. "I suppose twenty years of you-know-what doesn't make any difference. And don't pretend you don't know what I'm talking about, that it doesn't exist."

Billy looked down at his hands. It was like a nightmare going on inside him and outside him at the same time. His head felt as if it was full of scrambled eggs.

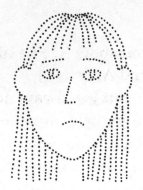

9 The Ghost of Rena O'Hara

But finally Billy's father went upstairs to change his clothes to go to the office. He left the swinging door to the hall open. Rena had gone. But her face had left bulges in the screen. It was like the ghost of Rena O'Hara was still looking at him.

His mother was scrubbing the sink as if *it* had been arguing with her. Emily was playing with her doll.

Bulges in a screen weren't a ghost. Besides, ghosts didn't exist anyway. Rena had probably just been nervous like Amy. It was weird she was Joe's sister. She must have *looked* weird, red criss-crosses all over her face, even her lips. Wait till he told Joe . . .

Billy realised it could have *been* Joe . . .

somehow . . . he and Alan . . . they'd got Rena and Amy to . . .

But Joe always acted so gross around girls. He never paid any attention to his sister in school or the few times Billy had been over at their house. Joe was a year older than she. They were in the same grade, though, because he'd been sick in first grade. And Joe was about a foot shorter than Amy Miller.

And Alan was worse. If he accidentally bumped into a girl in school, he wouldn't even look at her; he'd just gather up his books and keep going. He wouldn't be in it if it had anything to do with girls. In square dancing he'd kept getting so mixed up Mrs Presser had finally just let him run the record player.

But then that meant Amy had really wanted him to go to the dumb dance with her?

10 How to Fight a Girl

"What difference does it make?" Joe yelled at Rena. "You didn't get him to *do it!*"

"It wasn't our fault," said Rena stubbornly, glancing at Amy. "Billy's weird. Amy told you what he said to her, that he was taking his grandmother to the dance, and with me he had orange juice all over his face. He's weird. So it wasn't our fault, so you still have to pay us what you said."

Amy kept wishing she hadn't gotten into it. Boys your own age always acted so stupid. Billy had probably known all along it was a trick. Maybe she should tell Rena she had to go help her mother. She didn't want to stand around all day listening to them argue.

"If you *don't* pay," hissed Rena, "I'll tell Daddy."

She and Joe glared at each other, waiting to see what the other was going to do, and then Joe suddenly made a break for the door.

Rena grabbed his arm and fell down, yelling at Amy.

"Door! Lock the door!"

Amy slammed herself against it, fumbling with the bolt. Joe wrenched free. Amy turned to face him, pressing back against the door.

"Watch out!" threatened Joe. "You think I care if you're a girl?"

But he didn't dare try to wrestle her out of the way. He wasn't sure where it was all right to wrestle a girl. Every time he even touched Rena now, she said she was going to tell Mommy he'd tried to grab her where you weren't supposed to. And Amy wasn't even his sister. He kept feinting at her, pretending to grab her, yelling, "If you don't get away from that door . . . ! You better! You better!"

But Amy didn't move, though her lips were trembling. Joe stopped yelling.

From behind him Rena said, "If you even touch her, you're going to be so sick".

Joe flinched. He'd forgotten about her. But she was all twisted around trying to see the back of her jeans. Amy was still glaring at him, pressed back against the door. If they ganged up on him, Rena wouldn't care what she did to him, she was his sister. And Amy wouldn't care what she did to him, she wasn't his sister.

"Oh." Rena sounded like she was going to cry. She touched the grease spot on the back of her jeans. "They're *ruined*. Now it isn't just paying us for *Billy*!" she screamed at Joe. "You're going to have to buy me a new pair of Calvin Klein's!"

"Rena, you can probably get it out with Mr Jiffy." Amy went to look closer.

Before either of them knew what had happened, the door was open and Joe was gone.

"I'll tell Daddy!" screamed Rena.

11 Fibs of All Kinds

"But then won't he tell your father and mother about what we did to Billy?" said Amy.

Rena picked up a cloth from the floor and began to rub the back of her pants. "Yeah. I know." She'd already decided it would be better just to tell her mother she'd fallen down.

"I better go," said Amy. "Mr Jiffy would really probably get it out. If you don't have any, I could bring ours over. Call me?"

Rena nodded, still scrubbing at her pants. Amy left. Rena decided the spot was almost all gone. So if she could persuade her Mommy to buy her new pants, she'd have these *and* new ones. . . . She decided that would be a sin she'd have to confess and then Father Jacoby would make her give the new pants back. But probably she'd never be able to get these really clean anyway. She began to look for other dirt spots. She still wasn't sure Billy hadn't been making fun of her when he'd come out of the kitchen with the orange juice all over his mouth, when he'd pretended they'd called him Eleanor. The few times he'd been around when Joe had made fun of her, like calling her Piano Legs or something, he hadn't laughed. He'd just watched. But she'd never been sure he hadn't laughed later. That's why she'd mushed her face against the screen, so he wouldn't think he could start making fun of her.

12 Jelly Jam

After he'd cleaned up his room, Billy decided to go see if Tom had come back from his grandmother's yet. At least then he'd have him on his side if Joe and Alan had gotten Amy and Rena on theirs. He went downstairs. He still couldn't believe it. He'd been partners with Amy once in square dancing. But he couldn't remember if anything had happened. It had been the day Joe'd kept falling down on purpose all the time, so everybody had mostly been watching that. Billy looked out the kitchen window. For some reason the backyard looked almost sinister – as if the two dish towels hanging on the clothes-line meant something, like a warning.

*

Amy stopped at the beginning of the little path through the weeds behind the motel. Rena had said it was a short-cut her brother and his friends used, so it must be all right. There weren't any windows in the back of the motel. She went slowly on. After it left the motel, the path followed an old stone wall. She came to some sheds and an old barn. Through some sumac she could see a backyard with a pool, then a garage and house. That must be Billy's house like Rena had said. Amy pushed her hair back from her forehead. She was already perspiring. Everybody ganging up on Billy wasn't fair – except it was probably his own fault. He always acted stupid, pretending to disco, boop-boop. She felt her forehead with the tips of her fingers to see if any perspiration pimples were starting; her mother said perspiration didn't cause pimples, but Rena said it did. Maybe she-should spy on him, see if she could catch him doing something dumb. Then if he said anything about yesterday, she'd have something to say back. She snuck through the sumac, ran around the still, silent pool, and stopped behind the garage to catch her breath, even though she hadn't been running that fast.

Billy pretended to feel the dish towels on the line. Glancing around, he began to feel silly. Nobody was spying on him. He broke into a run, jumped to touch the lowest leaves of the maple, and rounded the corner of the garage just as Amy bent down to peer around it. Her head butted into his stomach. He staggered back and fell down, clutching his stomach. She staggered back, holding the top of her head with both hands, not straightening up.

"What are you *doing*?" Billy clambered up. It was a girl. She was all bent over, holding the top of her head.

"What am *I* doing?" she said. "What are *you* doing?"

"It's *my* garage."

"It isn't *your* garage. You don't own it. Your parents do."

Billy was going to say it was more his than hers, but then he realised it was Amy Miller. Without straightening up she began to comb out

37

her long blonde hair with her fingers. Then she reached down and started to fool with one of her shoelaces. And then all of a sudden she straightened up with a jerk, tossing her hair back.

"It's none of *your* business what I do," she said.

She didn't have any weird makeup on and her hair was all loose, so she didn't look like Miss Disco Weirdo; she just looked like – like herself. On her pink T-shirt, in curvy red letters surrounded with little clouds, it said Love's Baby Soft.

Billy shrugged. "I guess I didn't expect someone to be there, here. You know, behind the garage."

She tossed her head back so her hair glittered in the sunlight.

"Did it hurt you?" he said. "I've got sort of a hard stomach." He bonged his stomach with his fist. Then he blushed.

"No, I was just going over to . . . to . . ." She pointed vaguely. She could feel her face getting all red. She tossed her head back. After yesterday, if he didn't know about Rena and Joe, he might think she'd been hiding behind his garage because she really liked him or something.

"Yeah." She looked like Brooke Shields. Of course, she didn't really. But she looked like someone who like went to the same school as Brooke Shields. He remembered she still might be on Joe's side, against him. She didn't look like it. He realised suddenly the only way to find out was to keep talking to her.

"Maybe she's not home," he said.

"Who?"

"Who you were going to see."

"Oh. Yeah."

They looked at each other.

Amy knew he couldn't really believe she'd been going to see someone and just happened to bend down to tie her shoe or something behind the corner of his garage.

Billy kept trying to think of something else to say. But she kept tossing her head back, so he felt like he was trying to talk to someone who kept pushing him, trying to start a fight. He pretended he was concentrating on picking what was left of the blister on his hand. He felt all jumpy, like he was scared that something *good* was going to happen. The only thing he could think of to say was that he couldn't think of anything to say. He started to bite at the last little nub of blister skin and then remembered she was probably watching him.

"What are you going to have for lunch?" she said suddenly, tossing her hair back.

"*Lunch*? Oh. Oh, I don't know. Peanut butter and jelly?"

Then she was looking at him as if she expected him to say something else. He finally understood.

"What are you going to have?"

"I think I'll have peanut butter and jam. Have you ever had peanut butter and raisins?"

"No. My little sister's friend eats peanut butter and bacon."

"My aunt eats peanut butter and bananas."

So they had a whole conversation about peanut butter and all the things you could have with it. Potato chips, marshmallows, chocolate, sliced tomatoes. Isn't it awful when it sticks to the roof of your mouth? French fries, bologna, sardines, canned peaches. Some kinds aren't good for you because they have too much sugar. Pickles, scrambled eggs, coleslaw, cheese. No, I like crunchy better than smooth. (After that disagreement, they both felt it was more like a real conversation.) Sauerkraut, tacos, 7-Up, Coke, Sprite, Tab, Pepsi, a glass of water, two glasses of water, *three* glasses of water, *four* glasses of water, *five! six!*

By then they were both laughing . . .

But then all of a sudden neither of them could think of anything more to say about peanut butter. Amy tossed her hair back. Billy knew she must be thinking how stupid he was for not being able to talk about anything but peanut butter. But he wasn't the only one. Why was it only him who was supposed to think up stuff to talk about? She wasn't saying anything either. She just kept tossing her head back like she thought she was some kind of *horse* or something. What was he standing around with a girl for anyway, when he could be doing something interesting like riding his trail bike? Mom had taken it away. So maybe if he explained to her that this *girl* wanted to try the bike, she'd let him have it back – just for the morning – because it'd be sort of women's lib like she was always so hot about.

13 The Ruin of Love's Baby Soft

Amy just watched at first. The track up through the field was even muddier than usual from the rain the night before. The trail bike slithered and slid under Billy, almost falling; he had to sort of wrestle with it. Mud spattered up on to the visor of the helmet; he was sweating. His jeans got so caked with mud they felt like the leather pants real motorcycle racers wear. Finally, when he stopped at the bottom for about the fifth time to wipe the mud and fog off his visor, Amy said well, maybe she'd try it now.

The first couple of times up and back Billy ran beside her. He could see she felt like he had the first time he'd ridden: the helmet bouncing every which way in spite of the chin strap; you're afraid you're going to get the brake and gas mixed up; you don't know how hard to squeeze the brake; if you stop too fast, you might catapult over the front.

But then about the third time up the track Amy left him behind; he couldn't keep up. At the turn-around at the top he saw her stick her inside foot out, then get scared and draw it back. But when she got heading down the track again, she gunned it and crouched way forward. She wasn't really doing it right; she was flattening herself too far forward between the handlebars so her rear end stuck up. But she was going as fast as Tom or Alan ever had. When she took off the helmet, her face was all red and sweaty, strands of hair sticking to her forehead and cheeks.

"Okay, your turn," she said, out of breath. Her jeans and T-shirt were spattered with mud.

She didn't remind him of Brooke Shields any more. But she looked even better somehow. There were little drops of perspiration on her upper lip.

*

44

They took turns after that till Amy decided to try a wheelie. Billy could see her pulling back, the front wheel coming up a little . . . But then the bike was starting to go out from under her sideways! It had happened to him: you felt as if the bike was all of a sudden disappearing like magic. She hit on her side, the bike slithering and bucking away like a wounded animal through the hay and daisies. It reared up and flipped over.

When Billy got to her, she was sitting up, shakily trying to get the helmet off. When she did, her face was all white. He and Joe had tipped over lots of times, but she was a girl; if she got hurt, Mom and Dad *would* make him sell it.

"You all right?"

She didn't say anything; she was trying to get up. He didn't know if he should help her from behind under the arms like a boy. Finally he just held out his hand. She pulled herself up and walked around a little, rubbing her leg.

Billy said, "The first time you fall, it shakes you up".

She nodded. Then she looked around for the trail bike and asked if it was hurt. Billy tried it, revving the motor. She wiped some of the mud off her hands and side with grass. Her whole side was covered with it; her Love's Baby Soft T-shirt was ruined. Billy figured maybe she'd go now. But when he pulled the bike up beside her and said it was all right, she said, "I guess it's like with a horse. You should get right back on".

And after a while Billy only remembered she was a girl when her T-shirt hiked up in back a little so he saw her bare skin or when she stopped to tie her hair back with an old piece of string he had gotten her from the trail bike toolbox. It was almost more fun than with Tom or Joe or Alan; she didn't argue all the time. They decided to make a turn-around at the bottom of the track so you wouldn't have to stop to turn around there either. They started to clear away rocks, piling them on to the stone wall.

And then Joe's sister Rena suddenly stood up on the other side of the wall and said, "Are you having a good time, traitor?"

She turned and went off through the field.

Amy looked at Billy, then at the rock she was carrying in both hands. Then she dropped the rock right on her foot, but started away through the hay anyway, limping so badly she almost fell down at every step. But at the top of the field she began to run and disappeared down into the orchard.

14 Billy Worm and Amy Beetle

Joe dropped his soda can into the wastebasket beside his mother's sewing machine.

"You want another?" he said to Alan.

"No."

Joe hadn't told Alan what had happened with Billy yet. Not that it had been his fault it had bombed out. Stupid Rena and Amy.

The kitchen door banged. Joe heard Rena say something. Footsteps came up the hall. He grabbed Alan and pushed him into the closet, pulling the door shut behind them. They heard the couch creak as if someone had flopped down on it.

"Little Amy Model," sneered Rena's voice. "She's so *disgusting*. She's supposed to be so *beautiful*, so interested in *acting* and *modelling*."

Her voice became angry. "But the first *boy* who comes along . . ."

Joe peered through a crack in the door, but he couldn't see who she was talking to. She was slumped on the couch with her hands shoved down into the pockets of her jeans. She put both her legs up on the arm of the couch. Then she hitched awkwardly around, her hands still in her pockets, till her feet were up on the back of the couch and her head was hanging down upside-down.

"Somebody should get her *and* him," she said after a while. "If Joe wasn't so disgusting . . ."

Joe realised she was talking to herself; she must have had a fight with Amy – like about Billy. Joe reached up and knocked three times on the inside of the closet door.

Rena squirmed wildly around and sat up. But after a moment she flopped back, calling to her little sister in the kitchen to see who was at the back door.

Joe knocked three times again. Rena sat up again. Then she suddenly charged off the couch. The closet door thudded.

"She's trying to lock us in!" Joe flung himself at the door and managed to force it open a crack. Rena was yelling to their little sister to come help. Joe heaved with all his might, the door slammed open, Rena fell over backwards, yelling that Joe was a sneak, she'd tell Mommy he'd been spying. But then Joe told her, come on, she said she wanted to get Amy and Billy, so did he and Alan.

"How?" said Rena suspiciously.

"I still haven't got it all figured out, something that gets both of them."

"They're so lovey-*dovey*," sneered Rena, getting up and examining herself to make sure her jeans and blouse hadn't gotten torn. "She was riding his dumb motorcycle all afternoon. They're so disgusting. She bites her fingernails. She only bites one finger at a time because she thinks that way no one will notice. And Billy eats worms. Billy Worm and Amy Beetle."

A door slammed in the kitchen. Joe and Rena's little sister and brother began yelling. Joe and Rena went to separate them.

Back in the closet, behind the coats, Alan

decided he'd just sneak away and go home. Rena always called him Four Eyes because of his glasses. Girls were stupid.

But then he couldn't get the front door unlocked, and while he was trying to figure out how to open one of the big window doors in the dining room, Joe saw him from the kitchen.

15 An Unnameable Creature from Mars

While they made hero sandwiches, Joe worked out the new plan. It didn't have to be that different from the first plan. He laid slices of onion on the cream cheese. Except now they wouldn't have to pretend Billy liked Amy. Or that she liked him.

"Hand me the salami. So we pretend we're them all over the mall; we write their initials in hearts all over." He traced a heart in the air with a slice of salami. "BF loves AM. And then" – Joe laid on lettuce; it was going to be so great, the new plan *and* this hero – "after we've spread around all these clues of how they're madly, passionately in love" – he spread mayonnaise thickly on the lettuce – "sloppy, gooey in love – so gross . . ."

He leered around at Rena and Alan, licking mayonnaise off his fingers. "Then" – he dotted the mayonnaise with olives – "we start dropping hints. Saying, 'Did you know Amy Miller spent a whole afternoon *riding Billy Forrester's trail bike*?' Or: 'Boy, yesterday I saw Amy Miller and Billy Forrester wearing each other's *T*-shirts!' And we write anonymous letters to their *grandmothers*." Joe began to spoon cold spaghetti sauce on to his hero. " 'Dear Grandmother Forrester: If you think your grandson William is such a nice boy, why was he necking with a girl in the movies like a gross slime?' "

Joe laughed so hard spaghetti sauce dribbled all over the counter and floor, down into the crack between the counter and the refrigerator, into the sugar bowl.

Rena just watched him. If he ever started to tease her about something, she'd have this.

"Geez. Okay." Joe wiped his eyes, getting mayonnaise on his eyebrows so he looked like a white-haired old man. "Okay. So it all starts to come out. But see, Billy and Amy aren't going to know what's happening. Like they're going to say we didn't do that, and see, they didn't, but other people aren't going to know that. And the real stuff they've done, like with the trail bike, will get mixed up with the stuff they didn't do." Joe embedded slices of tomato in the spaghetti sauce. "So pretty soon everything's going to be all mixed up. Their grandmothers'll be calling their mothers." Joe buttered the top of his sandwich roll. "'Ah jus' don't know what's going on; Amy used to be such a nice girl.'"

He mashed the top of the roll carefully down. "It's going to be so great." Picking up the hero, he opened his mouth as wide as he could and bit down on one end – the hero's insides glooged out the other end like an unnameable creature from Mars.

Alan had gone, slipping away with his thin, meagre hero while Joe and Rena argued about the mayonnaise which might have gotten on her blouse when Joe had lunged for a plate to catch the insides of his hero. Finally Rena had given up and taken her open-faced hero on a tray into the living room to watch TV.

Joe ate the insides of his hero with a fork, now and then taking a bite of the roll. It was depressing – like a dumb grown-up *salad*.

But it didn't matter. A hero was just a stupid sandwich. Getting Billy and Amy was still going to be so great.

16 Smacking Sounds

And that night, across town at the movie theatre in the Canfield Mall, Joe knocked on the window of the ticket booth, a New York Mets cap pulled low over his eyes, and said to the woman, "We can't enjoy the movie because two people are making noise."

The woman followed Joe into the movie. He pointed.

"That boy and girl are kissing so loud, nobody can hear."

The woman listened. Even through the thunder of stampeding cattle from the screen, wet smacking sounds could be heard.

The woman herded Rena and Alan in front of her out into the lobby. "All right now – "

Alan and Rena turned to face her. Alan's cheeks were covered with red lipstick lips. Rena was wearing spangly sunglasses.

"I know what their names are," said Joe behind the woman. "She's Amy Miller and he's Billy Forrester. They're always doing stuff."

The woman took off Joe's Mets cap so she could see his face. "What's going on here?"

"Nothing." Joe squinted up at her.

"All right, out," said the woman. "All of you. Go on."

"I didn't do anything," said Joe.

"Out. Go on. All three of you. Some of your stupid kid tricks."

17 All Alone Together

It had been raining all morning. Billy had slid up the two big doors of the garage and turned on the lights. Now and then he stopped polishing his trail bike to watch the water dripping from the roof, sluicing down the windshield of the car parked out in the driveway. It was so dark outside it was almost like night. The rain drumming on the roof muffled the scrape of his shoes on the cement floor, the click of the kickstand. But inside he was safe as long as the wind didn't start up. He heard running footsteps.

And then Amy was standing in the side door staring at him as if she'd just seen a ghost, rain dripping from the hood of her red rain jacket.

"They're trying to get us!"

Her story tumbled out. Last night she and her parents had gone shopping at the Mall and when they were leaving, they'd seen Rena and her brother Joe and his friend, that Alan Phelps, coming out of the movie theatre, and Alan had had lipstick lips all over his face – Amy blushed – and Rena had had on sunglasses – like a disguise?

Amy was all excited. Billy didn't say anything; he just watched her. She was probably just trying to trick him. Yesterday, while she'd been riding the trail bike, she hadn't acted sneaky; he'd even forgotten all about Joe and Alan and all that. But then when Rena had called her a traitor, she'd run away. So she could have just been interested in trying the bike. He'd never found out why she'd been hiding behind the garage. Watching TV with Emily after supper, he'd decided the whole thing was stupid. He just wouldn't pay any attention to it, just stay around and work on his bike for the next few days so it'd be all ready when Mom let him have it back. By then Tom would probably have returned from his grandmother's.

Now Amy was telling about how, driving home from the Mall, she'd begun to notice initials spray-painted on those mailboxes at the corners of streets on the wall of that old factory on Weaver Avenue. So then she'd known what the others were doing.

She stopped abruptly and just looked at him, sort of squinting a little. He didn't understand about the initials. Did she mean Joe and Alan were spray-painting initials all over?

"What initials?"

"Mine," said Amy. "Yours."

Billy still didn't understand.

"You know, like in hearts?" she said. "With arrows?"

"Oh. Yeah."

Amy wished she hadn't come. "So, see, they're all against us. They're trying to make us look dumb."

She untied her hood and, pushing it back, she shook her head to loosen her hair. She tossed her head. Then she looked around as if she was interested in the garage. She went over to the workbench and pretended to read the Workman's

Compensation notice tacked over it. Billy fooled with his polishing cloth, watching her. She had shorts on under her red slicker. Her legs were already tan. Just because she was supposed to be the prettiest girl in the class didn't mean she wasn't still trying to trick him. He said suddenly, "You mean it's like when you were in it with them?"

She didn't turn around. She just kept looking at the notice. The rain drummed on the roof. Then she said, "Yes. But I decided it wasn't fair for everyone to gang up on one person".

After that it was almost like when they had been riding the trail bike. They had to decide what to do. Amy had never been alone on a boy's side before; she kept hesitating, wondering if she was acting all right. Billy kept getting distracted; he'd notice something like her eyes were really blue, or he'd begin to wonder why her nose seemed so nice when it really wasn't that different from Alan's or Tom's. Finally they decided the best thing was to try to find out what the others were going to do next. Amy said she had to go home first because she hadn't told her mother where she was; besides, the rain. They agreed to meet behind the 7-Eleven store across the street from Joe and Rena's house as soon as it stopped raining.

"It's raining so hard now it's almost scary."

They watched the rain pelting down out in the driveway.

But finally Amy said, "Well, I guess I better go". She ran off down the driveway.

She even ran nicer than a boy. Billy remembered Joe and the other boys making fun of how the girls ran in gym.

18 Frogs

But while Amy was hurrying to dry her hair and change – just after she had gotten home the rain had stopped – her mother came in with some laundry and noticed her wet clothes on the floor.

"Amy, you didn't tell me you went out. When it was raining like that?"

"I had to see Rena." Amy combed her hair forward over her face. She couldn't say she'd been to see a boy; Mom always made such a fuss about boys.

"What about?"

"Nothing."

"I'll bet it was about last night and those two boys."

"That was just Rena's brother and his friend."

Amy hoped she wouldn't remember the lipstick lips on Alan Phelps's face.

"Not about that one boy's beautiful cheeks?"

"Oh Mom, I told you, that boy's just a nerd."

Her mother laughed. "But one day" – she did a little dance step to the door – "nerds change into princes like frogs in fairy tales." She went out.

Amy was embarrassed. But trying to decide which shorts and T-shirt to wear, worrying she'd be late – if the others started off somewhere, Billy would have to follow them without her – it came over her that it was *like* going on a date. Of course, it wasn't. But Rena would say it was. That's what Rena and Joe and that Alan were trying to make everyone think. If Mom found out about it, she'd think . . . If someone like Janie Stewart found out, she'd tell everyone . . .

Amy sat down at her dressing table. If she didn't go, Billy might come to find out why and Mom would see him; she'd tell Daddy. Or Billy might get mad and persuade Rena and Joe to let him be on their side. So then they'd all be against *her*. Amy knew she'd be mad if someone who'd said they'd meet her didn't. It all made her mad anyway. It was like that women's lib person had said on TV; a girl and boy *couldn't* just be friends. So, was she going to just be like everyone else? If she didn't decide, it'd be too late to do anything.

Finally she decided to wear something weird, sort of almost a disguise; then if someone saw her, they probably wouldn't recognise her, but if they did, they'd know it couldn't be a date or anything – obviously in such weird clothes she was just fooling around. It was just like a game, she and Billy against the others, like in basketball. Which is what it really was. Amy looked through her closet. When you chose up sides in gym, it wasn't your fault if you got on a side with nerds. Sometimes people teased you, but that was mean; nerds had feelings, too. Not that Billy was just a nerd.

19 The First Date

Billy peered around the corner of the 7-Eleven store. Alan had gone into Joe's house about ten minutes ago, but since then only Joe's dog had come out. Maybe Amy wouldn't come. Even if she did, she probably wouldn't want to wait among all these smelly garbage cans. He glanced back up Houston Street. A girl in a big floppy hat had come around the corner of the Jewish Community Centre. He couldn't see her face, but it sort of looked like Amy. She had on a dress, not shorts like that morning. She came across the street. At the end of the driveway, which ran up the back of the 7-Eleven, she stopped and lifted up the front of the hat to look out, and Billy saw it was Amy.

"It's a disguise," she said. "In case they see us."

"Oh. Yeah. Nothing's happened at Joe and Rena's." A disguise? Billy peered around the corner again. The hat was so big, everybody would notice it. And anyway, nobody wore hats. She was like an ostrich, hiding her head in the sand. And the dress was shiny blue and all fancy-flouncy around the bottom. So the disguise was that she was pretending she was going to a party or out on a date?

Billy realised it was like a date. He glanced back at her. She was just standing there, like she was waiting for him to do something. He couldn't see her face under the hat.

Under the hat Amy was wishing she hadn't come. It was so hot and the horrible smell of garbage. She almost felt dizzy. She could feel her hair beginning to perspire. And she had this horrible sinking feeling that something was wrong. Maybe it was only that she couldn't see anything because of the hat. For all she knew, everyone from class could be standing all around her right now silently laughing and pointing at her because of Mother's gardening hat and her old fourth-grade party dress.

Peering around the corner, though he wasn't seeing anything, Billy realised that's why Amy was being so silent: she thought it *was* a date. So she was waiting for him to do something – whatever you were supposed to do on a date. He glanced back at her. She was still just standing there under the hat. It was like being on a date with a toadstool or Darth Vader!

A dog was barking.

Joe's dog. It was barking from the top of the porch steps. Billy realised Joe and Alan and Rena were already almost out of sight up Lockerman Avenue.

"Come on!"

He and Amy had to run to catch up, ducking behind parked cars.

20 Supergirl

From behind the corner of the movie theatre in the Canfield Mall they watched Joe and Rena and Alan disappear into the Grand Union across the parking lot.

"We'd better wait here."

Amy sat down on a broken concrete block. Someone had to have seen them running crouched all over all the way to the Mall. Not that she cared. What other people thought wasn't important. It was just that it was stupid. Yesterday with the trail bike had been sort of fun, but this was stupid, like little kids, hide-and-seek. She could feel her hair all clotted and sweaty under the hat. It had looked so nice, she'd really felt good, and now it was all horrible.

Billy kept licking his lips, glancing at her. She was just sitting there silently again. What did Miss Toadstool expect him to do? What did he care? Let her sit there. Girls were so dumb. With the trail bike and that morning in the garage she'd acted normal. He remembered her suddenly appearing in the door all excited, her hair curling out from under her red hood, raindrops on her cheeks and eyebrows.

Not even Joe or Larry Wilcox, like probably no one in any of the fifth grades, had ever done anything with a girl. Just like nobody but him had ever eaten a worm. And they'd all laughed at him about that, but they'd really wished they'd done it – even the grown-ups did – everybody really thought he was "a wild and crazy guy". At the movies like Brooke Shields's face got bigger and bigger and bigger till it was so huge . . . its lips open a little, teeth glistening. Kizzing. It'd only be like an experiment. It wouldn't mean he *liked* her. Just because you dissected a frog in science it didn't mean you hated frogs.

He turned stiffly, like Frankenstein, not letting himself really think about what he was going to do, and lifted the front of Amy's hat. Amy gazed up at him out of the dimness, her lips slightly parted, her face flushed. He kissed her. For an instant neither moved, their lips pressing together. Then they pulled back. They gazed at each other again.

And then she *shoved* him!

He tripped and fell over backwards. She was scrambling up, the hat falling off. Her blonde hair flashed in the sunlight. She tossed her head. Sprawled on his back upside-down in the dirt, sloping towards the drainage ditch, he gazed up at her – **SUPERGIRL, WONDER WOMAN,** looming, towering over him!

She turned and disappeared around the corner.

After a few minutes Billy sat up and looked around to see if anybody had been watching. Then he ran his tongue along his lips. Big deal. It hadn't been anything. Like kissing the back of your own hand. Maybe her lips had been a little softer, warmer . . . and he'd felt her – her teeth behind them.

Everything was so dumb. Crud.

21 The Slippery Cigarette

Joe and Alan and Rena came out the back door of the Grand Union and went along the back of the Mall. They were all wearing spangly sunglasses. Joe and Rena were arguing. Rena didn't think they should do it. They'd get in trouble.

"If Daddy ever finds out about us painting names on store windows – "

"*With whipped cream.* You could lick it off. Anyway it's only going to be empty stores." Joe took a tiny foil packet out of his shirt pocket and began to carefully unwrap it. "Anyway, nobody's gonna recognise us. We've all got sunglasses like Amy's."

"That's what you always say: it's going to

72

work, it's going to work. And then it never does. You always get in trouble."

"It worked in the movie, didn't it?" There was a cigarette in the tiny packet. "And now we're going to go around to a few stores so there'll be somebody besides the lady in the movie who can say they saw Billy and Amy acting lovey-dovey *and*" – Joe held up the cigarette triumphantly – "*smoking*. It's going to be so great." He leered. Then he set the cigarette carefully between his lips.

"If Daddy finds out you smoked, he's not going to care if it's whipped cream."

Joe struck a match. "All right, you – " He had to stop talking because it made the cigarette wiggle so he couldn't get the match against it. Rena and Alan watched him. The cigarette glowed. Joe puffed.

"Aw right, you go home 'f ya" – he had to talk out of the side of his mouth like a tough guy – " 'f ya don' like it. We don' need ya."

Smoke was getting up his nose; his eyes were smarting and tearing. It felt more like the cigarette was smoking him than him smoking it. He coughed. The cigarette shot out of his mouth and bounced off Alan.

"Crud." Joe shoved Alan and picked it up. "They're making these new cigarettes so slippery."

But after that he didn't try to smoke and talk at the same time. He concentrated on putting it between his lips, taking a puff, taking it out of his lips, blowing the smoke out.

"Okay."

They went down the alley to the front of the Mall. By the time they got there, Joe was puffing and waving the cigarette around like he thought he was some hotshot high-school tobacco fiend with his fingers stained all nicotine yellow.

"Okay. Okay. Now for them stores." He tried to tap the ash off the cigarette with his finger. The cigarette flipped out of his hand and bounced off Rena's arm. *"Come on! Geez!* What're you shoving me for?" Joe stooped to pick it up.

"Hey."

A high-school boy had come out of the alley.

"Aren't you too young to smoke?"

A high-school girl appeared behind him.

Joe straightened up, stepping back. He didn't see he was stepping off the edge of the sidewalk and stumbled, falling against two trash cans, knocking them over, the trash spilling. Alan and Rena fled toward the alley.

"Smoking's already stunted his brain," said the girl. She and the boy laughed. He ground the cigarette out with his sneaker. Then he unlocked the Video Gap. They disappeared inside.

Joe got up shakily in the trash. They didn't have any right to tell him what to do! They weren't even grown-ups! Something wet was sticking to his forehead.

A piece of bloody waxpaper?

He staggered. He was bleeding? He felt his forehead gingerly, noticing, geez, there were bloody French fries and bits of hamburger roll all around him in the trash. He looked at his finger. Then he smelled it.

It was ketchup.

In the depths of the Video Gap a light flashed. That high-school boy and his dumb girlfriend. She'd said he was stunted. They'd pushed him into the trash. They'd mashed the cigarette to nothing!

Yeah, and suppose they got their whole window whip-creamed? Joe ran, stumbling, towards the alley.

"Joe! Joe, you better wait till you calm down. You *better*! You know what Mommy says about losing your temper."

But Joe already grabbed the paper bag of whipped-cream cans and was running back down the alley. Rena and Alan glanced at each other and then fled the other way.

"He's going to get in so much trouble!"

Joe peered into the window of the Gap. The long narrow room, video games and pinball machines along each side, was dark and deserted; the weird revolving lights hadn't even been turned on yet. He began to spray whipped cream on the big window, back and forth, back and forth. When he'd sprayed as far up as he could reach, he peeked in the door and then darted inside, sprayed "Billy loves Amy" on the nearest pinball machine, then bigger, on the wall beside it, "Amy Miller loves Billy Forr – " He saw something move in the dark change booth in the back and fled

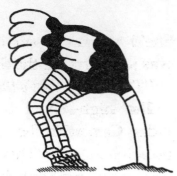

22 What the Ostrich Means

Just as Billy looked around the corner to see where Amy had gone, Joe ran pell-mell out of the Video Gap and disappeared up the alley. He was running as if someone was after him. But then nobody else came out of the Gap. Billy realised the big window of the Gap was covered with white gunk. Amy was way up at the other end of the Mall by the Grand Union. She was looking in a store window; she hadn't noticed Joe.

A man came out of a deli three or four stores from the Gap. His stomach stuck out under his T-shirt. When he got to the Gap, he stopped short. Then he ran inside, yelling, "Frankie!"

Amy had started back across the parking lot.

She'd put on a pair of spangly sunglasses and was just carrying the floppy hat.

"That's her! That's the girl!"

The high-school boy had come out of the Video Gap with the man in the T-shirt and was pointing at Amy. They both yelled at her to stop. The man ran out into the parking lot and grabbed her by the arm and started talking angrily to her. Billy ducked down and ran behind the cars to get closer.

The man was saying something about things being ruined, sprayed with gunk. Billy peered cautiously through the windows of the car. The man's face was all red. Amy looked like she was going to cry. He was trying to make her go back to the Gap with him.

Billy didn't know what to do. He couldn't just run away and leave her. She didn't even know what was happening, that it was probably whatever Joe and probably Alan and Rena had done. The man probably thought Amy was Rena. Lots of video game places were supposed to be run by the Mafia even. A man came out of the fish store near Billy with a white apron on.

"That's my sister," said Billy, pointing at Amy. "We don't even know that man."

"What?"

"That girl's my sister. We don't even know that man who's yelling at her."

The man with the apron grabbed Billy and yelled, "Lou, what's the matter? This kid says he's the girl's brother".

People came out of other stores. The man in the T-shirt turned out to be the owner of the Video Gap. He kept telling everyone how a gang of kids, these were two of them, had wrecked his place, sprayed gunk all over everything. A woman interrupted to say last night two kids had tried something funny in her theatre.

Billy and Amy kept saying, "It wasn't us. We haven't even been in there".

But Billy knew it had been Joe.

Somebody asked them their names. Amy said Amy Miller . . . she hadn't done anything, she'd . . .

Billy started to say his name but then remembered he'd told the man with the apron he was

Amy's brother. The owner of the Video Gap grabbed Billy.

"Forrester", he read from the name tag inside the collar of Billy's shirt. "William Forrester."

He didn't let go of Billy's shirt. Billy didn't dare look up. Now they wouldn't believe him even if he did tell them about Joe. They probably wouldn't do anything to Amy; she was a girl. But people didn't care what they did to boys; they might start punching and kicking him.

Beside him Amy suddenly said, "You'd better call my mother. She doesn't like people grabbing me".

And then she reached over and put the big hat on Billy's head. The man let go of his shirt. The hat was too big for him and came down over his eyes, so he couldn't see *anything*. But he somehow felt safer. Everyone was probably still staring at Amy. For the first time he understood what the ostrich means when it hides its head in the sand.

23 An Ugly T-Shirt

Amy's mother came. Billy explained to her how he'd seen Joe run out of the Gap. He didn't say anything about Rena and Alan or how they'd been trying to get Amy and him. Amy's mother took them to her car and then went to call Billy's mother. Amy sat in front, Billy in back.

After a while Billy said,

"I don't see how spraying stuff on a store window was supposed to 'get us'".

Amy didn't answer.

Billy didn't care. But if she was so mad at him, why had she put the hat on him? Billy saw his mother go into the Gap. A moment later she came back out with Amy's mother. They came across the parking lot to the car.

"Come."

Amy and Billy followed them to a little island in the middle of the parking lot with two benches and a dead tree.

"Let's sit," said Billy's mother.

Amy said, "Mom, I've never been in that place. That man hurt my arm. He – ".

"Amy." Her mother stopped her. Neither of their mothers was acting really mad. Amy's mother looked like she was trying to think of the best way to talk to them about something very, very serious. Billy remembered that once Joe had said something about Amy's mother being sort of weird, something about how she was always teasing Rena about her boyfriends even though she didn't have any.

"Amy," she said finally, "what happened in the game place is very serious."

"And it doesn't just involve Joe and his sister," said Billy's mother.

"Yes," said Amy's mother. "But we'll talk about that later. First I'd like to talk to you both about something that I think is even more serious. You know" – she glanced down at her hands, then up at Billy and Amy again – "liking someone is a very precious thing. It's something that involves all of us, not just our minds and feelings."

Billy felt as if he was starting to drown.

Amy said, "Mom, I don't like – ". She stopped; she'd remembered Billy could have just run away when the man had grabbed her.

"Amy, there's nothing wrong with liking another person," said her mother. "It's just that liking someone, wanting to be close to them, can sometimes run away with us."

She paused and just looked at Amy and Billy. Billy wanted to shrivel up to a teeny-tiny hard little nut hidden way deep down inside himself. She and Mom couldn't have found out about what happened behind the movie, the kizz.

"Sometimes it's better if we wait for things," Amy's mother went on. "Feelings are funny. We want to rush, rush, rush, rush." And then she started talking about "being mature", "waiting for feelings to mature", "because feelings mature, too. They don't grow tall or gain weight but . . ."

Billy stopped listening. Just the way the word

"mature" *sounded* was embarrassing. Ma-choo-your. Like manure. He concentrated on looking straight at Amy's mother without even blinking. If she or Mom thought he wasn't paying attention, they'd probably start all over again. He couldn't tell what Mom was thinking because she'd put her sunglasses on. Amy's mother had lipstick on one of her teeth. It was like she and Amy and Mom had taken off their shoes and socks – and made him take off his – and then everybody had put their bare feet up on the table and were discussing how they smelled and their toe lint and all. He couldn't believe it was happening.

And then he realised his mother was saying something to Amy. About Amy and him going to the movies?

Amy said,

"Mrs Forrester, I *couldn't* have been there. Mom and Daddy and I were shopping at Marshall's last night. In fact, we saw the others coming out of the movies."

Amy's mother nodded. Then his mother was looking at him.

"Billy? What do you think is going on?"

But he hadn't really been listening since Amy's mother had started talking about like uh – *feet*. He stared back at his mother, trying to think of what he could say so she wouldn't know he hadn't been listening. He decided he'd better just give up.

"I wasn't really listening. You know, all the time. I . . . I've got this . . . like something stuck between my teeth." He began to dig at his teeth with a finger, sliding down on the bench in case she grabbed –

But she just told him how three children had been smoking and the high-school boy who worked in the Video Gap had made them throw away the cigarette so they'd snuck back and sprayed whipped cream.

Billy started to interrupt to say it hadn't been him and Amy; he'd told Amy's mother – But his mother said wait, let me finish. She glanced at Amy's mother and then went on: it was his and Amy's names that had been written with the whipped cream and the woman who ran the movie theatre said last night a boy and girl

86

named Billy and Amy had been misbehaving in the movie, kissing.

"Mrs Forrester, I know what happened," said Amy. "It wasn't Billy and me. It was the others."

And then she explained, blushing, how Rena had been mad at her because Billy had let her ride his trail bike, but it hadn't been anything (she glanced at her mother), she'd never ridden a trail bike before so she'd just wanted to try it. So Rena must have persuaded Joe and probably that Alan Phelps to help her, like, get revenge.

Billy realised she was leaving out stuff, even stuff Mom might remember, like her and Rena coming to the house to ask him to the dance. But at least nobody had said anything yet about behind the movie, kizzing. He didn't even like to think a word like iss(k) or ug(h) with them all around him. And he was the only boy, too.

"Well," said Billy's mother when Amy had finished, "I think we had better go have a talk with Joseph and Rena. You know – " She paused. Then she said, "Billy". So he had to look up. "You know, you and Amy may not have been in the video game room when Joseph was doing what he did, but you were all involved in this together. It doesn't concern just Joseph and his sister and Alan."

Billy nodded. But he had begun to feel better. Nobody had said anything about behind the movie. He didn't care if he got blamed along with everybody else for the other junk. Besides, him and Amy couldn't get blamed that much for something they hadn't even known was happening. His mother went off to tell the owner of the Video Gap that they would be back very soon.

But waiting in the back seat of the car with Amy, Billy got that hollow sinking feeling again: Joe or Alan or somebody could have seen what happened behind the movie. So he'd just say what had really happened; it'd just been like eating another worm. He glanced at Amy. She was looking out the window. She reached up and pushed back her hair. He remembered riding the trail bike with her . . . and in the garage in the rain . . . how she'd gotten all dressed up to meet him. And then she'd put the hat on him to protect him. And suddenly he realised that even though she'd pushed him away when he'd like ——— her, she hadn't done it right away. She could have pushed him as soon as their lips touched.

They stopped at Amy's house so she could change into sensible clothes. When her mother had asked her why she was wearing a dress, she'd said just for fun; it had just been part of the other stuff. Her mother hadn't noticed the hat. So everything would be all right as long as no one had seen Billy try to kiss her. Not that it mattered. *She* hadn't done anything, only stupid Billy. Of course, Rena would still say she had. Mom had talked about how feelings are funny. Amy remembered the trail bike.

She rummaged angrily, hopelessly, through her T-shirt drawer again, not caring if she rumpled *everything*. She just didn't have *any* T-shirts that didn't say something like Dreamboat or Love Me Love My Dog.

"Amy," called her mother from downstairs. "We're all waiting."

Finally she just took a plain ugly turquoise

one. It even had a purple stain on it. She looked in her top drawer for a rubber band for a pony-tail. Last year in camp she and Laura Stanes had practiced kissing the insides of their elbows; it was supposed to be the part of you which was the most like lips. But it hadn't been like that at all with Billy; it had been ... She stopped twisting the rubber band around the ponytail, trying to remember exactly what it had felt like.

"*Amy!* We're waiting."

She ran downstairs. When she saw Billy, he somehow didn't look anything like she'd ex-pected, like she'd been remembering. He looked so much smaller, dingier, ordinary.

24 The Way It Looks Isn't the Way It Is

When they got to Joe and Rena's house, Joe hadn't come home yet. Billy's mother explained to Mrs O'Hara what had happened. Billy saw Rena listening at the top of the stairs. Finally Mrs O'Hara called her down, and they came out on the porch. Mrs O'Hara didn't know what to do. She kept saying Joseph was a good boy; sometimes he got excited, but he wouldn't do anything bad.

"Is there any way to reach Mr O'Hara?" suggested Billy's mother. "This may be something you'll want to discuss with him. It's really very serious. We were only able to persuade the owner not to call the police by promising to get everything cleaned up right away."

Alan crawled out from under the porch. "I was with *her*." He pointed at Rena. "We didn't do anything." He blinked up at them. The police? They were going to get arrested?

Billy saw Joe peeking at them through the windows of one of the cars parked along the sidewalk. A moment later he limped out from behind the car. Billy could tell he was faking. He'd smeared dirt on his cheeks.

Joe admitted he'd lost his temper and sprayed a little whipped cream around. But he'd only done it because that high-school boy who worked in the Video Gap had pushed him down in the trash to show off in front of his girlfriend.

Amy kept saying her arm still hurt where the man had pulled her; she'd never even been in that place. Billy could tell her mother was beginning to be more on their side. But his mother was still just watching. Then she suddenly asked Joe why he had written Amy and Billy's names in the whipped cream.

Billy almost stopped breathing. If Joe had seen them behind the movie, he'd say something now.

Joe looked sheepish. "Yeah. Well." He

shrugged. Then he glanced at Amy and Billy as if trying to tell them if they'd just keep quiet, everything would be all right, nobody would get in trouble. "It's just everybody – everybody sort of thinks Amy and Billy are like, you know, like they're good friends."

"That's not *true!*" Amy looked like she was going to hit him. "It's only because you and Rena and that Alan Phelps were trying to make it *look* that way, saying we did things we never even thought of."

"We didn't start it," said Joe.

"You *did!*"

But Billy could see Amy didn't really believe it.

Joe shrugged. Nobody else said anything.

"Well," said Billy's mother. Billy could tell she wasn't sure what was going on. "Well, for now we had better just go back to the Mall and clean up the mess. Then we can try to get to the bottom of all this."

When the clean-up was finished, the two mothers lined them all up outside the Gap, and the owner came out, and they said they were sorry, and he said well, it had been a crazy thing to do. He hoped they'd learned their lesson. He'd be glad to see them in the Gap anytime as long as they behaved themselves.

"I like kids," he said to the two mothers. "That's why I'm here, to entertain kids."

"And make money," whispered Joe.

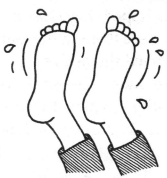

25 Real Feet

At Billy's house, after they'd all gotten out of the car, Billy's mother said, "All right, now Mrs Miller and I want you all to go out by the pool and talk everything over among yourselves. And when you've talked everything over, we want you to come back and tell us what was going on. We want you all to recognise that this was very, very serious. That man would have been perfectly within his rights to just call the police."

At first nobody said anything; everybody just stood around looking at the pool. Billy was afraid Joe might start teasing him about Amy. Amy decided if Billy thought she was still really mad at him for doing what he'd done behind the movie theatre, he might say she'd let him do it. Of course, she was still mad at him – or she wasn't mad at him. She just thought he was stupid. Finally Rena said she wasn't going to get in trouble for something she hadn't done. She was going to tell her father. He'd punish the people who had really done the stuff Mrs Forrester was talking about.

So Joe pushed Alan and said he was going to punch Rena; she'd done everything anyone else had.

Amy said, "We shouldn't argue with each other. We have to figure out what to say to Mrs Forrester and my mother."

"Yeah," Billy said. "They said it didn't matter if Amy and me weren't there, we were all like in it together anyway."

"I don't think they're going to do anything more to us as long as we admit we were wrong," said Amy.

Joe suddenly grabbed Alan by the throat. "Down on your knees! Confess! Confess!"

"Cub on," croaked Alan.

So everybody laughed, and then Billy said,

"Look, we'll *write out* a full confession and everyone sign it". That way it'd show his mother and Mrs Miller they were really serious about it.

"Like we really *understand* what we did wrong," sneered Joe.

Amy and Billy both thought Joe was almost sort of making fun of their mothers, but Billy only said, "Yeah. So okay?"

Amy nodded. Rena and Alan didn't say anything. Billy went off to get paper and a pencil.

"All right." Billy pulled a chair up to the table by the pool. "Now first we list all the stuff everybody did, like what you were doing and what Amy and I did to try to find out what you were doing. One." He started to write. "Amy pretended she was asking me to the dance. Two. I said no, I was taking my grandmother because she could disco so well." Billy jumped up and pretended to disco, making fun of himself.

"And three," said Amy. "I thought he was crazy and tripped over the doorsill I was in such a hurry to get away." She stumbled wildly around.

"And Joe smoked!" said Alan. He pretended he was trying to light a cigarette about a yard long, his whole arm shaking and trembling.

"Yeah, and then that crud knocked me into the trash – " began Joe.

"He didn't knock. You just backed off the sidewalk yourself." Rena was laughing so hard she could hardly imitate how he'd looked. Even Joe had to laugh.

"Yeah and after," he said, "when I got up, there was something stuck to my forehead. So I thought . . ."

Pretty soon they were all laughing and staggering around. Billy kept writing, even though he was really laughing, too, because until they got the confession written and signed, and everything settled, there was still a chance somebody would get mad or something.

"OKAY!" He held up the paper. "Done. Now everyone sign. Amy Miller." He handed her the pencil. "Joseph Q. O'Hara. No, don't really sign Q."

Rena and Alan signed. Billy signed last. "*Okay!*"

And then he felt so good. They all felt so good. Alan was still staggering around imitating Billy and Joe and himself. But nobody else knew what to do. And then Billy suddenly said, "But the part we haven't put down – the part you don't even know about – is when Alan pretended he'd drowned!"

And he pushed Alan into the pool even though he had all his clothes on.

And then he jumped in himself.

And then Joe did.

And then Joe and Billy climbed out and grabbed Rena to drag her in. She screamed. Amy hugged her around the middle to try and stop them. But neither she nor Rena were really trying that hard. Everybody was yelling and laughing so hard. It was all mixed up.

SPLASH!

And then Alan climbed out to put his glasses somewhere safe, and the others thought he was trying to get away, so they all chased him and got him down, even Amy and Rena. Then they dragged him back to the pool and swung him by the hands and feet, everybody pushing and shoving and falling down.

"One, two, *three!*"

Amy and Joe fell in, too. Billy dove in and swam underwater and grabbed Amy's ankle. Rena was running around the pool not letting Alan out, screaming to the others to help. But when Joe tried to push her in, she flopped down and hugged the diving board. Amy started to climb out to help her, but Alan, who was taking off his wet sneakers and socks by the ladder, suddenly stood up stiffly right in front of her, his face getting all red.

Amy hesitated. She looked down at herself. Then she just let go of the ladder crossing her hands over her chest, falling backwards. Billy thought she was pretending to be a corpse, so when her head came up, he pushed her down again. Then he saw she was really choking. She groped for the ladder with one hand and hung on, coughing, her other hand still across her chest as if she'd hurt herself or something. Rena sat up on the diving board.

Finally Amy choked out, "Rena. Your . . . your T-shirt".

At first Billy and Joe and Rena didn't understand what she was talking about.

Then they all realised at the same time: when your T-shirt's wet, you can see through it. And it sticks to your skin.

Rena rolled off the diving board almost on top of Billy. But he was already diving down, swimming underwater to the other side, thinking desperately:

REAL feet!

He clambered out of the pool and kept going, not looking back. Joe was ahead of him already, almost to the garage. He suddenly started to run. If his father ever heard about this. . . .

But when Billy got around in front of the garage, he hesitated. Where was Alan? Billy couldn't see the pool. He didn't want to yell to him. Finally Billy ran crouching into the garage and peeked out the back window. It was so dirty he couldn't really *see* anything, just vague shapes. Alan was gone. Rena and Amy were still in the pool, just their heads above water. Billy couldn't hear what they were saying. They weren't saying much. They kept looking around, pushing their wet hair back off their foreheads. Pretty soon Billy could tell they were beginning to shiver.

Then Amy disappeared behind the edge of the pool and suddenly reappeared climbing the ladder! She was heading right for him! Billy ducked down. But she'd folded the bottom of her T-shirt up over the top so her stomach was bare above it, where like uh her *feet* were, there were two layers of T-shirt, so it didn't look like anything, just T-shirt.

Suddenly Rena ran past her with both arms crossed over her chest. The screen door slammed. Billy ran to the front of the garage. Amy was dashing up the back steps. She grabbed the screen door open, tripped over the sill, and fell flat on her face into the kitchen.

26 Hello Goodbye

Billy knocked on Tom's kitchen door. But Tom still hadn't come back from his grandmother's. Going home, Billy realised he'd turned up Fair-lawn by mistake. But he could cut back around by Elm Street. Maybe his mother wouldn't make him wait another day for his trail bike if he told her there was no one around to hang out with. Alan had already started his summer school course; Joe helped his father every summer. Billy glanced across the street at Amy's house. Mom would probably let him have the bike with Amy like before. Yeah, and then if Joe found out. . . . And it'd be starting it all up again with Mom and Dad; they'd thought the confession was so funny; it would almost have been better if they'd just punished him. Amy was probably over at Rena's or some other girl's house anyway.

From the window of her room Amy saw Billy walking by across the street. She wondered if he was going home to ride his trail bike. If her mother saw him, she'd say something like oh, there goes your boyfriend. Amy sat back down at her dressing table and looked at herself in the mirror. Finally she decided to make herself up like a twenty-first-century TV star.

"All right," said Billy's mother. "Because you weeded the flower garden so carefully this morning."

Billy got a shovel out of the barn and worked for half an hour, smoothing the ruts in the steepest part of the track. The first time he tried it, gunning the bike full out, it felt as if he was taking off when he hit the top. Like flying! He'd land somewhere way off over the hills and far away in Pennsylvania! The bike hit, he managed to pull it around the curve, down around the old stump, up over the root bump – like a real motorcycle racer.